little Miss Stubborn

by Roger Hargreaves

D0267438

Little Miss Stubborn was, as you might imagine,
extraordinarily stubborn.

Once she had made her mind up
there was no unmaking it.

If she decided to go out,
she went out.

Even when it was pouring with rain!

One Sunday, when it wasn't raining,
she decided to take the bus
to Mr Strong's house.

Why?

Because she had run out of eggs.

And, as everybody knows,
Mr Strong always has lots of eggs.

As the bus arrived, Mr Nosey walked by.

Being nosey, he couldn't help asking:

"Where are you going, Little Miss Stubborn?"

"To Mr Strong's house," she said.

"But this bus doesn't go anywhere near there!"

But Little Miss Stubborn took the bus anyway.

And you won't be surprised to hear it didn't
go anywhere near Mr Strong's house.

It went to Coldland.

A country where it is so cold
that everybody has a cold all year round.

"What a charming place!" she said, shivering
and trying to look as if she had really planned
on coming to Coldland in the first place.

Which of course she hadn't.

As you know.

She ran along a path to keep warm.

"ATISHOO!" somebody sneezed all of a sudden.

It was Mr Sneeze.

"If I were you," he warned, "I wouldn't
take … ATISHOO! that path. It's icy! ATISHOO!"

"I'll take it if I want to!" snorted
Little Miss Stubborn.

And she followed the path.

But can you guess what happened?

WHOOOOOOSH!

She slipped on the ice!

"That was fun!" said Little Miss Stubborn.

But of course it wasn't.

She came to a fork in the path.

"I shall go this way," she said,
taking the right hand path.

"You're making a big mistake!" said a worm,
popping his head through the snow.
"This way isn't safe."

"Don't be silly!" cried Little Miss Stubborn
and started off down the path.

She should have listened to the worm!

Before she had gone very far
an avalanche of snowballs fell on top of her!

One of the snowballs rolled off the path
and rolled and rolled down a very steep hill.

And, inside it,
Little Miss Stubborn rolled and rolled
down the very steep hill as well.

The snowball rolled a very long way,
all the way into a different country
where it melted.

As luck would have it,
Little Miss Stubborn found herself
outside Mr Strong's front door.

She was soaked to the skin.

"My goodness! You're wet through!"
said Mr Strong.
"Quick, come in and dry yourself
before you catch a cold."

"I don't catch colds," said Little Miss Stubborn.
"Anyway, I've come for some eggs.
Out of my way!"

"That's no way to behave," said Mr Strong.

"Rubbish!" snorted Little Miss Stubborn.

Still wet through,
she marched into Mr Strong's kitchen.

Without a please or a thank you,
she helped herself to a large bowl of eggs.

"You could at least ask," said Mr Strong.

"ATISHOO!" sneezed Little Miss Stubborn.

"I told you you'd catch a cold," said Mr Strong.

"I don't catch colds," said Little Miss Stubborn,
and sneezed again, "ATISHOO!"

She was so hungry by this time
that, there and then, she made herself
an enormous omelette.

It was gigantic.

It was so big that it won't even fit on the page!

Then she began to eat her enormous,
gigantic omelette.

And the more she ate, the more worried
Mr Strong became:
"You'll make yourself ill," he said.

"Fiddlesticks," snorted Little Miss Stubborn,
and because she was who she was,
she finished that enormous, gigantic omelette.

And there is not much more to add.

Other than now you know how
extraordinarily stubborn
Little Miss Stubborn is!

Stubborn to the very end ...
the very end of this story.

CUT ALONG DOTTED LINE AND RETURN THIS WHOLE PAGE

3 Great Offers for MR.MEN Fans!

MR.MEN TOKEN

1 New Mr. Men or Little Miss Library Bus Presentation Cases

A brand new stronger, roomier school bus library box, with sturdy carrying handle and stay-closed fasteners.
The full colour, wipe-clean boxes make a great home for your full collection.
They're just £5.99 inc P&P and free bookmark!

☐ MR. MEN ☐ LITTLE MISS (please tick and order overleaf)

2 Door Hangers and Posters

In every Mr. Men and Little Miss book like this one, you will find a special token. Collect 6 tokens and we will send you a brilliant Mr. Men or Little Miss poster and a Mr. Men or Little Miss double sided full colour bedroom door hanger of your choice. Simply tick your choice in the list and tape a 50p coin for your two items to this page.

PLEASE STICK YOUR 50P COIN HERE

Door Hangers (please tick)
☐ Mr. Nosey & Mr. Muddle
☐ Mr. Slow & Mr. Busy
☐ Mr. Messy & Mr. Quiet
☐ Mr. Perfect & Mr. Forgetful
☐ Little Miss Fun & Little Miss Late
☐ Little Miss Helpful & Little Miss Tidy
☐ Little Miss Busy & Little Miss Brainy
☐ Little Miss Star & Little Miss Fun

Posters (please tick)
☐ MR.MEN
☐ LITTLE MISS

3 Sixteen Beautiful Fridge Magnets – any 2 for £2.00! inc.P&P

They're very special collector's items!
Simply tick your first and second* choices from the list below
of any 2 characters!

1st Choice

- [ ] Mr. Happy
- [ ] Mr. Lazy
- [ ] Mr. Topsy-Turvy
- [ ] Mr. Bounce
- [ ] Mr. Bump
- [ ] Mr. Small
- [ ] Mr. Snow
- [ ] Mr. Wrong
- [ ] Mr. Daydream
- [ ] Mr. Tickle
- [ ] Mr. Greedy
- [ ] Mr. Funny
- [ ] Little Miss Giggles
- [ ] Little Miss Splendid
- [ ] Little Miss Naughty
- [ ] Little Miss Sunshine

2nd Choice

- [ ] Mr. Happy
- [ ] Mr. Lazy
- [ ] Mr. Topsy-Turvy
- [ ] Mr. Bounce
- [ ] Mr. Bump
- [ ] Mr. Small
- [ ] Mr. Snow
- [ ] Mr. Wrong
- [ ] Mr. Daydream
- [ ] Mr. Tickle
- [ ] Mr. Greedy
- [ ] Mr. Funny
- [ ] Little Miss Giggles
- [ ] Little Miss Splendid
- [ ] Little Miss Naughty
- [ ] Little Miss Sunshine

*Only in case your first choice is out of stock.

---TO BE COMPLETED BY AN ADULT---

To apply for any of these great offers, ask an adult to complete the coupon below and send it with the appropriate payment and tokens, if needed, to MR. MEN CLASSIC OFFER, PO BOX 715, HORSHAM RH12 5WG

- [ ] Please send _____ Mr. Men Library case(s) and/or _____ Little Miss Library case(s) at £5.99 each inc P&P
- [ ] Please send a poster and door hanger as selected overleaf. I enclose six tokens plus a 50p coin for P&P
- [ ] Please send me _____ pair(s) of Mr. Men/Little Miss fridge magnets, as selected above at £2.00 inc P&P

Fan's Name _____

Address _____

_____ **Postcode** _____

Date of Birth _____

Name of Parent/Guardian _____

Total amount enclosed £ _____

- [ ] **I enclose a cheque/postal order payable to Egmont Books Limited**
- [ ] **Please charge my MasterCard/Visa/Amex/Switch or Delta account** (delete as appropriate)

| | | | | | | | | | | | | | | | | | | | | | Card Number

Expiry date __/__   Signature _____

Please allow 28 days for delivery. Offer is only available while stocks last. We reserve the right to change the terms of this offer at any time and we offer a 14 day money back guarantee. This does not affect your statutory rights. Data Protection Act: If you do not wish to receive other similar offers from us or companies we recommend, please tick this box [ ]. Offers apply to UK only.

MR.MEN   LITTLE MISS
Mr. Men and Little Miss™ & ©Mrs. Roger Hargreaves

CUT ALONG DOTTED LINE AND RETURN THIS WHOLE PAGE